Starlight glimmer

★★★ and ★★★

the Secret Suite

Written by G. M. Berrow

Little, Brown and Company
New York Boston

Little, Brown and Company

Hachette Book Group
1290 Avenue of the Americas, New York, NY 10104
Visit our website at lb-kids.com

Little, Brown and Company is a division of Hachette Book Group, Inc.
The Little, Brown name and logo are trademarks of Hachette Book Group,
Inc.

First Edition: August 2016

LCCN: 2016944258

ISBN 978-0-316-26631-4

10 9 8 7 6 5 4 3 2 1

RRD-C

Printed in the United States of America

For magical Mary-Kate,
who always has the missing
piece to my spells

CONTENTS

★ ★ ★

CHAPTER 1
Over Booked   1

CHAPTER 2
There's a Friendship Lesson
in Everything   11

CHAPTER 3
Starlight's Suite   25

CHAPTER 4
The Hyper Boost   33

CHAPTER 5
Light-to-Light   43

CHAPTER 6
The Shortest Journey Ever   57

CHAPTER 7
The Slow Down   65

CHAPTER 8
Comet Tail's Curse   73

CHAPTER 9
Snack Attack   79

CHAPTER 10
Short and Suite   87

CHAPTER 11
The Accidental Vortex 97

CHAPTER 12
Dragon Knows Best 105

CHAPTER 13
The Ponyville Game Night Parade 111

A SPECIAL SURPRISE 119

Chapter

1

Over Booked
★ ★ ★

The sound of Starlight Glimmer's hoofsteps echoed through the cavernous hallways of the Castle of Friendship. As she wandered the endless corridors, gliding from room to room, she was amazed that even after all this time living within its confines that there were still new areas to explore. Starlight was not used to having this much space—especially living with Twilight. It almost felt eerie, like she might be lurking around a corner waiting to jump out and surprise her at any moment.

Not that she was *afraid*. Starlight Glimmer was one of the most powerful magicians in Equestria! She had proven that her natural skills were a force to be reckoned with, but unfortunately her intentions were what needed some work. Starlight Glimmer needed to learn that magic wasn't supposed to be a means of controlling other ponies. Which was precisely why she had come here to Ponyville—to learn about the properties of friendship's powerful magic from Princess Twilight Sparkle. Also, to make new friends. Starlight struggled a little more with *that* one.

"What's this?" Starlight muttered to herself. The lavender Unicorn pony stopped in front of a mysterious door. She narrowed her eyes. It was different from the other shimmering golden doors in this wing. This one was a drab brown. Starlight looked to her left, then her right, before using her magic to crack the door open. From the ceiling to the floor, from the back to the door—books everywhere!

"Great Griffon's beak!" Starlight said, rolling her eyes and chuckling. "Another room of books? I'm beginning to think this is all an elaborate practical joke!"

"No, no," Twilight called out, popping her head over Starlight's shoulder. She laughed nervously. "I just use this room as storage for the books I'm gathering for the new library at Mythica University! Since they've invited me to come dedicate it, I thought it would only be proper to come bearing gifts." Twilight trotted inside, eyes full of stars. She grinned at the stacks like a dragon guarding its pile of treasure and gems. "It sure is something, isn't it?"

Starlight suppressed a smile as her eyes scanned the titles up to the top of a stack. "Definitely *something*." She wondered if the new librarians at the University planned on stocking any books of their own. At this rate, there might not be any room left on the shelves!

"Oh, there it is!" Twilight said, magically plucking a title from the bottom of the stack. She made sure to gently lift the others up so they didn't come tumbling down. "*Moon-curve's Guide to Interval Incantations.* I've been looking for this everywhere. It relates to your next friendship assignment—making time spent with your friends count!"

Starlight raised her brow. "Oh really?"

"Yes, I've got it all planned out for later this evening." Twilight said, a grin forming on her muzzle.

"Another lesson *today?*" Starlight tried not to appear upset.

"When you're done doing whatever it is you were doing." Twilight frowned. "It wasn't important, was it?"

"No, not really…"

"Great! See you in the throne room in fifteen minutes," Twilight replied. "I'm going to make us some healthy snacks. It could be a *looong* night of learning!" She giggled happily and trotted back to the door with a renewed pep in her step. The Alicorn looked back over her shoulder. "I know I say it all the time, Starlight, but I just love having you here in the castle so much. Having friends near just makes everything *better*, doesn't it?"

"Yeah." Starlight sighed with a smile. "So much better."

Starlight did mean what she said, but Twilight Sparkle's genuine excitement for teaching Starlight Glimmer always threw her off. Since Starlight had been so untrustworthy herself in her past life, she was still learning to accept other ponies' intentions. The old Starlight Glimmer (the one who'd controlled an entire town by stealing their cutie marks) would have been suspicious that all of this nice behavior was just in service of a plan to trick her. But it wasn't. The princess truly wanted to help her. It was kind.

But there was also a major problem with Twilight's unrelenting dedication to Starlight's friendship education—it was extremely exhausting.

Starlight yawned and snuggled against a pile of books and rested her head on the top one, entitled *Weather Formations: Meanings and Significance in Pegasus Culture*. A cloudy thought crossed her mind before she fell fast asleep. If Starlight could find a way

Chapter

2

There's a Friendship Lesson in Everything

★ ★ ★

The throne room table was covered with pages of notes and diagrams, with half-nibbled carrot sticks and cupcake wrappers littered amongst them. The old spell book lay open in the center of the mess, though it was practically present only for show at this point. The two ponies had read it so many times since last night that Starlight could recite it verbatim. But Twilight was still hyper-focused.

The Alicorn leaned in close to her scroll, scribbling furiously and biting her lip as she cross-checked it with the book. Starlight sat across from her, idly twirling a quill from hoof to hoof and staring at the wall. The words of the spell kept repeating in her head. It was starting to drive her mad.

"Aha!" Twilight exclaimed, causing Starlight to jump. "If we add a phrase to the second verse of Mooncurve's Minutiae spell, by *literally* stretching it, we can achieve our desired effect! Minutes will feel longer, but the actual time will be unaffected. I don't know why it didn't occur to me before."

Twilight shook her head in amazement without tearing her eyes off the page. "And if we get it right in the next three days, we'll be able to use it on one of the most fun nights of the year—Ponyville Game Night! What do you say, Starlight? Want to give it a try right now?"

"Not really," Starlight admitted with a nervous laugh. "The minutes have felt pretty long as it is, you know?"

"What?" Twilight looked up and the study haze lifted. "After all our work you don't even want to give it a try?" Twilight chuckled. "That's just silly."

"Totally joking." Starlight looked down, feeling sheepish. Twilight could tell that she was holding back her opinion. The last thing Twilight wanted was for her student to feel like she couldn't speak her mind. When Twilight had something more to say, Princess Celestia always knew.

Twilight bit her lip hesitantly. "Is everything okay?"

"Well…" Starlight met her eyes. "Can I be honest?"

"Of course!" Twilight exclaimed. "Honesty and communication are cornerstones of friendship. Just ask Applejack or Pinkie. She named the actual cornerstones of this castle 'Honesty' and 'Communication'! But she also named one of them 'Sea Otter,' so maybe I shouldn't mention it—"

"I just need some alone time!" Starlight blurted out. Her cheeks flushed red with embarrassment as Twilight's face fell. She hadn't meant it to sound so rude.

"Just to . . . *take a nap*," Starlight assured. She pointed her hoof at the piles of work on the table. "All this studying has made me really tired. I don't know where you get your energy, Twilight."

"Of course it has." Twilight nodded, her frizzy mane swaying gently. "I'm sorry." She looked like she could use some sleep, too. Twilight sighed. "Sometimes I get so excited about studying that I forget to pace myself. Go take all the rest time you need." Twilight laughed. "Besides, it will be here when you get back!"

"Not unless you solve it first!" Starlight encouraged with a wink.

"*Mmm hmm,*" Twilight mumbled back, already buried in her book again. Starlight had barely stood up from the table before

Twilight was once more mouthing the words to the spell she was trying to alter.

Starlight had spent a mere twenty minutes in her room before she'd grown restless. Flopping onto the cozy four-poster bed and burrowing into the covers wasn't enough to center her—the truth was that she wasn't actually tired. All the hours that Starlight Glimmer had spent with Twilight staring at spells in books, trying to decipher meanings, had given her a sense of deep fatigue and mental fogginess. She was used to working by herself, and all of the studying would have wiped her out as it was, but the collaboration was extra draining. After staring at the pattern of ceiling tiles for far too long, Starlight decided that perhaps a trot was all she needed to get her brain working again.

The pony hoisted herself up, touched her hooves to the ground, and set off for another jaunt around the castle. Starlight hummed a tune as she took a familiar route, turning left instead of right, traveling away from the wing where she had been the day prior.

Suddenly, Starlight came to a halt as she noticed the same brown door from before—the one that led to Twilight's room of books for the University.

"That's odd," she said aloud. "I could have sworn this room was in the opposite wing…" There were no others like it in the castle; she was positive. Starlight shook her head as if to clear the confusion. Her mental map of the space must have gotten all mixed up since she'd been working so hard.

Might as well go look through the books, Starlight thought. *There might be something to help us finish this spell.*

Twilight must have left a light on inside. There was a faint glow around the edges of the doorframe. As Starlight treaded closer, the light seemed to brighten. That wasn't normal. Starlight paused. She was about to open the door with her Unicorn magic when a voice startled her.

"Hey, Starlight!"

"Spike!" Starlight laughed. "It's just you. Good." She was embarrassed that she'd been so caught off guard that her heart had started beating faster, even though there was no way for the young dragon to know it.

Spike shrugged, popped a piece of emerald into his mouth, and crunched. "Who else would it be?" he said in between the loud bites.

"Twilight." Starlight looked around quickly and leaned in to whisper. "She's seriously so focused on the idea of us solving Mooncurve's time spell that we've been working nonstop together. If she knows I'm not *actually* in my room, she'll probably want my help again, but I think I'm more helpful on my own for a little bit." Starlight cocked her head. Her lavender and aqua mane fell to the side. "So don't tell her where I am, 'kay?"

"No problem, Star." Spike popped another gem into his mouth. He laughed and shook his head. "But if you want to be alone, you should probably just try and solve the spell yourself.

That way it will be done!" Then Spike turned on his scaly foot and left in the direction he'd come with a wave. "Just a suggestion though!" he called out.

Even though Starlight knew Spike was joking, she couldn't help but think he might be onto something. But where to go? Not her room or the library—that was for sure. If she wanted to complete the spell quickly, Starlight Glimmer needed to be somewhere in the castle where there would be no chance of Twilight finding her. The faint glowing from the book storage room caught her eye once more.

"A great place for a little time and space," Starlight mumbled aloud to herself. She reached out her hoof to shove the heavy brown door open, but it wouldn't budge. It had opened so easily the day before! Starlight frowned. Had Twilight locked it? Either way, Starlight now wanted to get inside the room even more desperately. She conjured up the turquoise magic aura from her horn and used it to thrust the door open.

A blast of rainbow light whooshed past her, blowing her mane back with the wind! Finally, when Starlight blinked the blindness away, the room before her was nothing like it had been before. Every single book was gone, and in its place was something far better. Starlight smiled as her head began to flood with a million ideas, scheming. "This will be my little secret," she giggled deviously as the door clicked shut.

The turquoise energy shot from her horn, formed into a heavy lock, and secured itself to the door handle. Little did she know, outside, the door sealed into itself as well, blending into the wall without a single seam to give it away. Starlight Glimmer had found her space, and now she was going to whip up some time. On her own.

Chapter

3

Starlight's Suite

✦ ✦ ✦

Starlight Glimmer still wasn't sure how it had happened, but the room had completely transformed from the packed book storage room she'd encountered yesterday. Twilight must have moved the donations for the University in the middle of the night!

Or perhaps a pony had come to pick them up early this morning? Whatever the case, this room was now a beautiful suite filled with all of Starlight's favorite elements.

"Where did all of this come from?" Starlight wondered.

As she trotted around, it occurred to her that she had been mistaken. There was no way this was the book storage room. It couldn't be. The structure of it was similar, but there was no way even Twilight could have changed all of this so quickly even with magic. This was a hidden room in the castle and *Starlight* had found it. All that exploring had paid off.

From the light sky-blue color of the walls to the soft carpet covered in pinprick stars that actually glowed when Starlight's hooves touched them, each detail of the den was tailored to her tastes. There was a pedestal for spell books and a velvet sofa for languidly lounging between conjures. There were swaths of gauzy fabric filled with tiny twinkling lights, and a small mirror pool in the center for reflecting. It was as if it had come from her mind, or maybe even an illustration from the biography of Star Swirl the Bearded!

"Am I imagining this right now?" Starlight reached out her hoof to the gilded spell pedestal. She gave it a light shove. It was solid. She smiled and breathed a sigh of relief. It was a real secret hideout, just for her! A rush of excitement flushed through her, thinking of all the things she might be able to cook up for Twilight. Now when the two of them met, Starlight would have some new ideas to bring to the table. She couldn't wait to get started.

A stack of blank scrolls on a large circular table beckoned to her. Starlight chose a quill from a wooden box filled with a selection of writing instruments and got right to it. *Mooncurve's Minutiae*, she scribbled at the top. Below, she filled in all the words she could remember from the book. She bit her lip in concentration as she began to alter the sayings and soon, time began to melt away.

Starlight awoke with a jolt. The surface of the mirror pool shivered. The golden sand in the hourglass floated inside. The scroll with the spell on the sofa next to her lay unfurled, shaking as if a breeze blew through the air, when in fact, there was nothing of the sort. The room was windowless. Starlight had clearly lost track of how long she'd been working in here. Starlight mumbled the last line of the spell to herself, slowly remembering where she was and what she had been doing. "From here to there...when transforms, then...the seconds to share...shall feel well spent."

She rubbed her eyes and looked again. The sands began to sift through the glass once more and the pool was calm. She yawned. It was time to go find Twilight Sparkle and spend some time with her. After all of her relaxing solo study time,

Starlight actually felt a twinge of excitement about seeing her new friend again. She was refreshed. And she actually *had* taken a nap, so she wouldn't have to lie to Twilight! She just might...omit some things.

As the pony crept out of the door of her hideout, she sealed it again with her magic energy lock. The turquoise light pulsated around it. It was so huge and bright that it lit up the whole hallway. Maybe it was too conspicuous. "I know!" Starlight removed the lock. "This will do the trick to keep my little room just for me." She conjured up some energy, shot it at the brown door, and watched as it became an identical gold color to the others in the hall. "Works for me." She nodded. Then the well-rested pony headed off to find her mentor for some new lessons in friendship.

"There you are, Starlight!" Twilight called out, her brow furrowed in concern. "Come sit down with us."

Instead of being greeted by just Twilight Sparkle in the throne room, Starlight was met by five more ponies. Fluttershy, Rainbow Dash, Pinkie Pie, Applejack, and Rarity all sat in their respective thrones. But not one of them was smiling—not even Pinkie Pie. Starlight felt a pit of dread in her stomach.

Chapter

4

The Hyper Boost

★ ★ ★

"Are you sure?" Twilight Sparkle paced the
floor anxiously. "The entire town experienced a hyper time boost except me?" The
princess shook her head in confusion as she
tried to make sense of things. It had to be

an effect of the spell she'd been working on, but that was supposed to *slow* things down.

"I can only speak for mahself," Applejack replied. "But there I was, standin' in the orchard and the feeling came rushin' over me. Soon I was kickin' my hooves faster than a greased jalopy on an ice luge. I couldn't stop!" Applejack smirked. "Not that I'm complainin', really. All my chores are finished early, I guess…"

Rarity nodded in agreement. "I experienced the same exact phenomenon!" Her almond-shaped eyes were wide with disbelief. "It was bizarre. But trust me—one does not want to rush an embroidered bodice. It came out quite wonky." Rarity shook her head. "Such a terrible shame."

Twilight looked at the others. "And you?

Did you experience an odd, faster-than-ponily-possible sensation in your activities? One that you had no control over but were aware of?"

"Oh yes," Fluttershy replied. Her face contorted into a look of distress. "I was flying and it was the fastest I've ever gone." She shook her soft, pink mane. "It was *awful*."

"Well, I didn't feel a thing!" Rainbow Dash declared. She puffed with pride, raising a sassy eyebrow. "But that's probably because I'm already faster than lightning."

"Pinkie?" Twilight prodded. "Anything?"

Pinkie Pie yawned. "I was taking a nap because I was tired from playing every single game ever in preparation for Ponyville Game Night, and I woke up and I felt like I hadn't slept a wink, even though the clock said I'd had at least *forty* winks, which didn't make sense at all! Plus, I'm so Sad Pinkie that I missed something as fun-sounding as a 'hyper time boost'!" Her bushy fuchsia mane was springing out in every direction. Her face turned to a big frown. "I guess you could say I'm ... *grumpy*."

Everypony gasped.

"Okay, that was pretty funny the way you all did that at the same time." Pinkie's frown exploded into a smile. She giggled. "Thanks, ponies. I'm feeling better now."

"Phew!" Twilight exhaled as she took a seat on her throne. "I was beginning to think I'd altered your personality again with my spell-bending in addition to all this odd time stuff."

Rarity and Applejack glanced at each

other with a shudder, remembering the strange events in which Twilight Sparkle had tried to complete Star Swirl the Bearded's spell. She'd ended up accidentally switching all of her best friends' cutie marks. Rarity still cringed at the thought of the hideous dresses Applejack had tried to sew and the horribly misguided weather patterns she herself had tried to create using Rainbow Dash's true talents.

"Spell-bending is extremely risky work—it takes very advanced magic and it's unpredictable." Twilight surveyed the mess of papers and books that still littered the table in front of them. "I should have done more research on this one first. I just wish I knew what went wrong!" She riffled through the papers and bit her lip.

Everypony nodded sympathetically. Except Starlight, whose mind had already wandered back to her new secret hiding spot. "Right, yes. Me too!" Starlight chimed in when she noticed the others' eyes on her. "Maybe you didn't recite the words slowly enough?"

"Hold up, now. You weren't here working with Twilight, sugarcube?" Applejack looked at Starlight a little sideways. "I thought the two of ya were busier than a coupla barn rats in a rotten apple heap with all that studying!"

Starlight opened her mouth to answer but before she could, Twilight interrupted. "No, no. It was all my fault." She looked down with a sigh. "Starlight *was* working with me earlier, but we were working for so long that she was exhausted. During the hyper boost she was in her room taking a nap."

"Hey!" Pinkie squealed. She put up her hooves in the air then pointed them at Starlight with a smile. "Nap twins!"

Starlight suppressed a chuckle and trotted over to Twilight. Her mentor was visibly upset. If Starlight had learned anything about friendship so far, she knew that right now she was supposed to be offering friendly support or viable solutions.

"Don't worry, Twilight," Starlight assured, putting on her best, confident smile. Her purple eyes sparkled with sincerity. "I'm ready to hit the spell books again, if you want! Whatever went wrong, I'm sure all of us can fix it together." Starlight looked around to each of the ponies (and dragon) at the table. "Right, everypony?"

A murmur of agreement filled the room. Pinkie Pie, Fluttershy, Rarity, Rainbow Dash, Applejack, Twilight Sparkle, and Spike always looked after one another—no matter what happened!

A look of pride washed over Twilight's face. "Thanks, Starlight, that's all I needed to hear." She smiled at her student. Even though she still had a very long way to go, Starlight had learned so much about friendship in such a short amount of time. The princess couldn't help but wonder what capabilities she might be able to uncover in Starlight if they had even more minutes in the day together.

Twilight glanced down at the scribbles

on the scroll. Her new version of Moon-curve's Minutiae danced around on the page, taunting her. She knew she ought to just try to solve the hyper time boost problem and file the spell away for good. But when the sudden thought of Comet Tail's Curse came flooding into her mind, even though it was just an old ponys' tale, Twilight knew she had to finish what she'd started or face dangerous consequences.

Chapter

5

Light-to-Light

★ ✶ ★

Twilight Sparkle and Starlight Glimmer waved to their friends as they exited the castle doors. After a little deliberation, the plan they'd decided on was simply that each pony monitor her own area of Ponyville and report back if anything strange in the way of time warping happened again. In truth, there was not much more they could do.

Starlight Glimmer had just stepped hoof in her bedroom quarters to gather some items to take to her secret suite when she heard something outside.

"Pssst!" Twilight whispered, poking her pink-and-purple mane inside Starlight's door. "Just came to, *uhh...check in.* Do you have a second to chat?" Her voice sounded high and nervous.

Starlight Glimmer hesitated, clenching her jaw in mild frustration for a moment. Friends were supposed to listen to one another, she reminded herself. Twilight deserved somepony to listen.

"Sure, Twilight. Take a seat," Starlight replied with a genuine smile. She waved her hoof toward her aqua-colored wingback chair. "Why don't you put up your hooves, too?" She used her magic to procure a matching fancy hoofstool. Then Starlight brewed a cup of steaming dandelion tea and placed it on the table next to her. "And a nice cup of this might help what is troubling you." Starlight wondered if she was laying it on too thick with the friendship gestures.

"Wow, thank you." Twilight fell back into the chair, clearly relieved. "What a day, right?"

"Definitely a day." Starlight nodded. She lifted her saddlebag full of magical accessories for the suite from the bed and placed it by the door so she could make a quick exit when Twilight was done. She was itching to visit the space again. She glanced back over at her guest, who was staring out the window with a frozen expression on her face. Twilight didn't look like she was going anywhere any time soon. "Are you all right, Twilight?"

"Me?" Twilight squeaked, her eyes bulging ever so slightly. "I'm just fine!" She was obviously fibbing. "I'm just excited for Ponyville Game Night. Have you ever played Settlers of Canterlot? It's so much fun but I never win. Applejack is the champion. I just hope this year I can finally beat her!" She let out a forced chuckle.

Starlight shot her a knowing look. "You're sure that's all you wanted to talk about?"

"Well…" Twilight took a sip of tea, avoiding Starlight's inquisitive gaze. "There is one other thing that's bothering me… relating to the spell."

Starlight Glimmer paused. She felt her stomach drop. Did Twilight know she'd been working on the spell alone? Did she know about the secret room? Deep down, Starlight knew she shouldn't have been snooping around the castle, and now she was caught! Her mind began to race. She'd be in so much trouble—Twilight would be so hurt. Perhaps once Twilight kicked her out of the castle for good, Starlight would find a home in Ponyville. Or go on the road with her best friend Trixie's magic act…

"There's just a lot of pressure sometimes, you know?" Twilight blurted out. The princess sat up and began to ramble. "After creating new magic the time when I altered Star Swirl's spell, then becoming an Alicorn and the Princess of Friendship as a result—everypony expects so much of me! I just really don't want to let ponies down. *Of course* I still want to study, create, and use magic, but in ways that help ponies have better friendship experiences so that everypony in Equestria knows what it's like to be supported by others the way I have here in Ponyville! But I know I have to loosen my grip and stop trying to control so much, like I did when you tried to bring Trixie to my dinner party. I think that's what Princess Celestia and Princess Luna meant when they replied to my last letter about learning to let go of—" Twilight stopped herself and sank back into the chair. "Oh! I'm sorry, Starlight. Listen to me! I'm supposed to be the teacher, not the clueless one. I didn't mean to unload all of this onto you."

So Twilight didn't know what she had been up to after all! She had truly just wanted to talk to her, as a friend. Starlight breathed a tiny sigh of relief and smiled. "Hey, don't worry about it, Twi. What are friends for?"

The two ponies smiled at each other.

"You're right," Twilight replied, taking a sip of her tea. "Thanks." She felt better already. But there was still one nagging problem that she'd yet to address—*Mooncurve's Minutiae*. The sense of incompletion bothered Twilight, like enjoying most of a perfect, crisp apple and then dropping the last bite of it in the dirt. "But we do have to finish what we started with the time spell. It would be horrible if we left it open and then we lost track of time! Hyper boosts at any moment! That would be awful." Twilight paused, eyes growing wide. "And have you ever heard of Comet Tail's Curse?"

"Don't tell me you seriously believe that silly little Unicorn's tale…"

"But what if it's true?" Twilight tried not to sound like a filly.

"Then I guess you and I will lose all of our magical abilities forever." Starlight laughed. "Yup, definitely going to happen."

"Starlight!" Twilight chided. "That's not funny."

"Sorry! But we're good, *trust me*," Starlight Glimmer assured. "Nothing else is going to happen. No more hyper boosts, no minutes-gone-missing, and certainly no weirdo curse bestowed upon us."

Twilight looked unconvinced.

"I know a lot about time-travel spells, remember?"

It was true. Back when Starlight had prepared her big evil plan, she had studied practically everything related to altering the timeline of events that led to Twilight and her friends ever meeting. Starlight and Twilight had followed each other through time and all over Equestria, which had been quite dangerous. But in the end, it had led them here—to being friends.

"How could I forget?" Twilight teased. She stood up from the chair and began to pace the room. Even with all Starlight knew about time travel, Twilight disagreed with her student that the matter of this specific spell was settled. It was of a different nature entirely—and if it wasn't dealt with soon, there could be dire circumstances.

"So what do you say?" Starlight grinned. "Let's just move on! I bet there are a million more friendship lessons just waiting for me to learn, right?"

Twilight regarded her spunky student. The ins and outs of friendship didn't always come easily to Starlight. She was still quite stubborn, and at times it was hard for Twilight to read her motivations. There usually seemed to be a secret agenda on her mind. For example, even as they spoke, Starlight had busied herself choosing items from her cabinet and carrying them over to a saddlebag like she was packing for a trip. What was that all about?

Twilight wasn't sure, but it did give her an idea.

"All right, then," Twilight conceded. She trotted over to Starlight's saddlebag and picked it up. "Your next friendship lesson involves your old pal, Sunburst. I want you to travel and visit the Crystal Empire for a few days. While you're there, you and Sunburst must rekindle an old friendship tradition!" Twilight grinned proudly. "Then you can start some new ones, too."

"Crystal Empire?" Starlight Glimmer's jaw dropped. *"Now?"*

"I noticed you packing and I thought that must be your little way of sending me a message." Twilight put her hoof on Starlight's shoulder. "Don't worry, I completely understand that you're exhausted from all this work you've done with me lately. You can go relax with Sunburst and learn about friendship with him for a little bit, then you'll be back just in time for Ponyville Game Night. It's going to be so much fun!" Twilight winked as she trotted to the door. "See you in a few days, Starlight!"

Twilight had to pat herself on the back for coming up with the perfect solution. She could focus on finishing Mooncurve's spell and closing the book on the whole problem—for good.

Chapter

6

The Shortest Journey Ever

★ ★ ★

Luckily, the kitchen was empty. Starlight crept around the corner and into the pantry as fast as she could. She scanned the shelves of food, grabbing as many provisions as she could without raising suspicions. Twilight would notice if too much was missing. She would be expecting that Starlight would eat her meals with Sunburst in the Crystal Empire.

Starlight tossed a jar of stewed peaches, some loaves of raisin bread, and three packs of cookies from Sugarcube Corner into her saddlebag. After reaching far into the back of the bottom shelf, Starlight was surprised to find a hidden bowl of glittering gems! "Spike, you sneaky dragon..." Starlight chuckled to herself. "Did he hide anything else back there? Aha!" she exclaimed in triumph, discovering a wealth of carrot jerky and sesame crackers.

It was a good haul—more than enough to sustain her for at least a few days while she hid out in her new secret room. Twilight would never even know she hadn't boarded the

Friendship Express that was now chugging its way toward the Crystal Empire. Instead Starlight Glimmer would stay holed up, figuring out *Mooncurve's Minutiae* herself.

Starlight felt so brilliant when the idea had occurred to her. Twilight was clearly worried about Comet Tail's Curse, that fake story meant to scare Unicorn fillies into finishing their magic homework. It would be an awesome surprise once she told Twilight that the spell was good and fixed. Perhaps her teacher would be so overjoyed and proud that she probably wouldn't even care that Starlight hadn't visited Sunburst yet.

Moving through the hallways of the castle undetected was much easier than Starlight had anticipated. It always seemed as if more ponies should be populating the place, rather than just the trio of herself, Twilight, and Spike. Her hoofsteps were loud as she galloped down the hall to find the secret door once more.

"One, two, three..." Starlight counted the doors as she trotted past, since she'd changed the color from brown to gold to disguise the one that led to her secret hideout. "Four, five, six...seven!" This was it. She used her magic to lift the handle, breath held with anticipation.

Starlight gasped. This wasn't her secret suite at all! It was just a simple guest bedroom. "No." She shook her head. "I must have counted wrong." Starlight backed out of the room and counted once more. It was definitely the seventh door. Starlight felt dizzy. Was it all just a dream before?

She was looking down at her hooves and

considering the options when her horn began to glow. Magic drifted from her toward the wall and a few seconds later, a loud creaking noise occurred. The doors magically began to slide down the hall like coats on a rack. They appeared to be making room for a glowing portal! Starlight was entranced. The radiant archway churned and sputtered drops of aqua-hued magical energy.

When it finally settled, there was a brand-new brown door in its place, just as before. Starlight Glimmer stood immobilized in shock for a moment. This was no ordinary hideout, like she'd thought. This beautiful room had come straight from her wild imagination and manifested itself into reality, appearing only for her.

"Even better." Starlight smirked as she

Chapter

7

The Slow Down
★ ★ ★

The Ponyville Town Square was almost ready. Colored lines delineating each team's home base were drawn with chalk on the ground and twisty, bright streamers in the same colors were swathed above. Pinkie Pie skipped and bounced as she tied yellow balloons in the yellow team section. "Are you excited, Rainbow?! I know I am!"

"Are you kidding? I'm pumped! Game Night is by far one of the most awesome nights of the entire moon!" Rainbow Dash called out as she flew up to the top of the flagpole. "It's almost like a mini Equestria Games, but a million times less pressure." She looped the official Game Day flag through the hooks and watched proudly as it billowed in the breeze. It bore a symbol of a rainbow color wheel, cut out like slices of a pie.

"Looking good, everypony!" From where Rainbow Dash was situated, she could see that the town square appeared as the symbol, too. Ponies busied themselves decorating in each of the colors and setting up boxes for ponies to hide behind during the big competition. She watched as Daven-port and Senior Mint worked on the green section, lifting a large crate from the Quills and Sofas shop into the center. It would make a great shield from the colored water balloons they were going to toss at one other.

Rainbow was about to soar down in a super-cool spiral and land in the blue sec-tion when all of a sudden, her wingbeats slowed. It felt as if the air was made of a thick goop that she had to push through. Rain-bow Dash winced in pain, spreading her blue wings wide and using all her strength built up from Wonderbolts training to stay afloat in the sky. *"Whaaaat...iiiis...haaaap-pening?"* she groaned.

At first, Rainbow thought it was just her,

but down below Senior Mint and Davenport were experiencing the same sensation! They grunted as they lifted the crate with their hooves, unable to move much faster than the slow crawl of a tortoise. It was like everypony and everything in town had been doused with molasses.

"Piiiiiinkie Piiiiie...." Rainbow called out. Her voice sounded really deep, like Fluttershy's did after touching a Poison Joke Flower. *"Whaaaaat* is *haaaaappening* to *uuu-uuus?"*

Pinkie Pie bounced over, the arc of her leaps slow and visible instead of the usual blur of pink and fuchsia. "I think it's Twilight's spell again!" Her voice was normal speed, which meant Pinkie Pie was probably attempting to speak in her hyper-fast chatter. "We'll never be ready for Game Night at this rate."

Rainbow's wings were moving even slower now. "I *thiiiiiink thaaaat's* the *leeeeast* of *ouuuur prooobleeems!*"

A blast of colored light exploded from the castle in the distance, spraying out through the town and returning everypony to normal. Having used too much force in her bounces to compensate, Pinkie Pie found her body launched and flying into the air. She landed on a pile of crates nearby. *"Whooooa!"* Pinkie Pie rubbed her flank with a frown. "Ouchies."

And for once in her life, Rainbow Dash wasn't expecting the burst of sudden speed and spiraled toward the ground, landing right on top of her pal. The two ponies looked at each other in concern, thinking the exact same thing. Rainbow Dash sprang to her hooves. "Come on! We have to tell Twilight right away."

"I'll be right behind *youuu*!" Pinkie Pie shouted.

The Pegasus and the Earth pony rushed off toward the castle faster than a hyper boost. And they would have gotten there, too, if time hadn't come to another screeching halt. All of Ponyville was trapped in slow motion, and there was no way to know when or if it would go back to normal ever again.

But Rainbow Dash and Pinkie Pie would keep trying to get to the castle until it did, even if it took them all week.

Chapter

8

Comet Tail's Curse

✶ ✶ ✶

It was worse than Twilight Sparkle thought! Until this moment, she realized she'd never actually seen Comet Tail's Curse; it had always just been a simple story passed on to young Unicorns. But there it was written in black ink on the page of a book. That made it more real than anything. She traced her hoof over the words: *The wizard who alters another's magic must see to its intended end, or prepare to see their magic come to an end.*

No more magic? What a horrible fate that would be! Twilight shuddered. As she went back to work on her scroll, she found herself wishing she hadn't sent Starlight Glimmer away. Solving this spell with a friend would be so much better.

Across the castle, Starlight Glimmer collapsed onto the pretty carpet of the suite. The Unicorn felt so dizzy she could barely breathe. This new version of *Mooncurve's Minutiae* she'd invented was incredibly intense. She'd tried to perform it so many times that she'd used up all of her energy. And it was all for nothing! Only once had it felt like something had shifted, but something was still off. According to her clock, time had not slowed back down at all.

Starlight stood up and stomped her hoof on the ground in frustration. "Why is this so hard to get right?"

Maybe this whole "hiding out" plan had been a mistake, thought Starlight as she trotted over to the sofa and reclined back into its soft folds. Starlight imagined an alternate reality in which she'd actually followed Twilight's instructions and visited Sunburst instead.

The two of them would have shared some Crystal berry pie while they caught up on Sunburst's new role as baby Flurry Heart's royal "crystaller." In turn, Starlight would have shared stories of her forays into friendship lessons and all the follies that followed them. He'd probably get a kick out of the time that Starlight had made friends with "the Great and Powerful" Trixie and become a magician's assistant. It sounded like it would have been a nice trip.

Starlight looked around the beautiful suite and suddenly felt very alone. But instead of wallowing in sadness or regret, she got back to what she was best at—making magic bend to her will. The Unicorn stood over the spell book and closed her eyes to concentrate.

The room began to brighten and whir, kicking up a tornado of wind around her. Items began to fly from the shelves and from her saddlebag on the floor as she recited the words. Excitement grew inside her. Starlight was finally getting it right! Twilight Sparkle and all of Ponyville would be so impressed when she showed them what she'd perfected. All she needed was a little bit longer to practice...and some more food.

Chapter

9

Snack Attack

★ ★ ★

It had been a lazy couple of days for Spike. Since Twilight was busy studying everything she could find about some random wizards named Mooncurve and Comet Tail, his best pony friend barely had any time to hang out with him. The irony was not lost on the dragon that the spell Twilight Sparkle was trying to complete in the first place was supposed to make it so that friends could have more time hanging out together. Still, Spike enjoyed his alone time now and then like anydragon else.

He'd spent yesterday reading through a bunch of his Smash Fortune comic books, then today he'd busied himself creating a new Oubliettes and Ogres character for himself. At his (and Big Mac's) special request, part of Ponyville Game Night this year was going to include a small tabletop tournament. Big Mac and Spike were really excited, and Discord would likely go all out, too, if he joined in the game. Spike just hoped the other ponies in town would take the game as seriously as they did. Either way, he would try to go easy on the poor unsuspecting newbies, but Spike made no promises.

Around noon, Spike's tummy began to rumble. Twilight was definitely too preoccupied to sit down and have lunch, and Starlight Glimmer was still on her assignment in the Crystal Empire, so he headed to the kitchen to help himself. Spike whistled as he walked, thinking of all the scrumptious snacks he'd stashed in the back of the pantry where nopony would find them.

When he arrived, he was shocked to discover that they were all gone! Well, except for the bowl of gems. But that was reserved for special occasions.

"Hey!" Spike whined, digging around. "Who ate all my good snacks?"

He reached for a piece of bread and tried to grab on to it, but he couldn't clasp his claws around it. It was floating! The magic that swirled around was a familiar aqua color, but...that couldn't be right. Spike cocked his head to the side in confusion and watched as the bread (along with a jar of peanut butter and some jelly) floated out of the kitchen door. "Not so fast, food!" Spike called out as he scrambled after them.

The dragon chased the potential sandwich through the halls of the castle, past the distracted Twilight, and even past his own bedroom. The food bobbed along as if it were alive. Finally, it arrived at a set of doors. But it didn't go in. Instead, the jars of peanut butter and jelly thrust themselves against the wall in between the doors repeatedly. A quick glance at his surroundings suddenly jogged Spike's memory. This was the exact spot he'd run into Starlight Glimmer just a few days before. She'd asked him not to tell Twilight he'd seen her!

Spike narrowed his eyes as he put two and two together. Starlight Glimmer hadn't gone anywhere—she was right here in the castle, somehow behind that wall. A glowing pulse started to light up the spot, and within a few moments, an aqua portal opened up as if it were curtains being tied back from a window. A brown door was revealed. It swung open and the enchanted food items bobbed their way inside.

Not only was Spike snackless, he now

Chapter

10

Short and Suite

★ ★ ★

"Spike, I really don't mean to be rude but I am extremely busy right now," Twilight said without tearing her eyes away from her book. Her pink-and-purple mane fell over her eyes. She blew it away with a puff of air. "Is everything okay?"

"No, Twi, it's, um…not." Spike's voice was small. He shifted from claw to claw and his eyes were darting around.

At this, Twilight sprang to attention with a look of genuine concern on her face. "I apologize for being so distracted." She was physically unable to ignore a friend in crisis. "Please, tell me what's wrong."

Spike hopped onto his throne. "All of the snacks are gone!"

"Spike!" Twilight exclaimed, looking more than a little annoyed. "That's your big crisis? You know you're welcome to go to the market and just get some more if you want to." She shook her head.

"Um, let me rephrase that." Spike rubbed his chin with his claw. "The snacks are gone and *I* didn't eat them!"

"Well, neither did I." Twilight rolled her eyes.

"Exactly. Somepony else did!" He put his claws on the table and leaned in. "Somepony named Starlight Glimmer."

The princess leaned her ear against the wall to listen for sounds of her student. The fact that Twilight didn't hear a peep coming from inside made her skeptical, but Spike had been so insistent that it required exploration. He wouldn't just make up the whole story for no reason.

"Here goes nothing!" Twilight readied herself. She closed her eyes in preparation. She felt weaker than ever from all of her attempts to finish *Mooncurve's Minutiae* before the Ponyville Game Night later. It took most of Twilight's remaining energy, but she gathered it up and aimed straight for the blank space between the two doors.

ZAP! A massive magic beam expelled from Twilight's horn. The glowing curtains of light parted once more. Sure enough, just like Spike had described, there was a brown door in its place. It slowly creaked open, leaking shafts of light into the hallway. It was too bright to see inside. The pony and the dragon squinted.

"Wait here, Spike!" commanded Twilight before galloping headfirst into the doorway. "I'll be right back."

The moment she stepped through the

doorway, Twilight Sparkle felt like she was being sucked into the room. Her body lurched forward and tumbled across the floor, then slid to the back wall of the room as if Twilight were a gigantic magnet. The Alicorn blinked her eyes, trying to get her bearings and gain purchase on the floor with her hooves.

"Twilight!" Starlight Glimmer's voice cut through the commotion. She came galloping up, bracing herself against the forces. "I'm so glad you're here!" Starlight reached out her hoof to Twilight and pulled her up. "I'm so sorry! I know I was supposed to be in the Crystal Empire! I didn't mean to—"

"Explain later!" Twilight interrupted. She scanned the room in a state of panic and confusion. Where had this place even come from? "We have to fix this . . . whatever it is!"

"I think I accidentally created a vortex!" Starlight cried out. Her mane whipped around in the worsening wind.

"Are you sure?" Twilight tried to step back toward the doorway, but she wasn't grounded enough. Vortexes could only be created with the strongest magical energy known to ponykind. Surely Starlight Glimmer wasn't that powerful on her own . . . was she?

"Look at it! What else could it be?" Starlight winced as a book flew past her head. "Swirling colors! A strong force sucking everything nearby into one central spot!"

There were bags under Starlight's eyes. Her appearance reminded Twilight of the way Princess Cadance had looked when she was trying to protect the Crystal Empire from King Sombra. It was the sign of a pony that'd been overdoing it on magic spells.

A bed from the room across the hall slid in through the door and slammed against the back wall.

"Okay, you're right," Twilight admitted. "It's a vortex!"

Starlight's eyes were fraught with panic. "What do we do?"

Twilight knew the answer, but it made her nervous given her current state of magical exhaustion. "We have to stop it with what started it—magic!"

Chapter
11

The Accidental Vortex

★ ★ ★

Pinkie Pie and Rainbow Dash had almost completed their arduous slow-motion trudge to the castle when time suddenly decided to speed up again. The two ponies slammed against the heavy front door as if they were being pulled against it. Rainbow reached out her hoof to try to pull it open but it wouldn't budge. The ponies were trapped like bugs on sticky paper!

"Look!" Pinkie Pie shouted in an impossibly high-pitched voice. She pointed her hoof back to the town and chattered superfast. "Everypony's-rushing-over-to-the-castle-I-wonder-why! And-all-the-stuff-for-the-games-is-flying-over-too! How-loony-rooney-is-that?!"

Rainbow could hardly believe it, but Pinkie was right. It appeared that everypony—and every *thing*—was headed straight for them! From game pieces and decorations for Game Night to teacups and carrots, nothing was safe from the strong force of attraction to the castle.

What in Equestria was happening here?!

Inside, the winds were picking up. Furniture from every area across the castle was now being pulled in the direction of the room. Spike hung on to the doorframe with his claws, his body horizontal. His little feet dangled in the air as he gripped tight. "Are you two going to do something or just stand around staring at each other?" he yelled over the cacophony of clangs and crashes. "Because my claws are kinda full!"

"Yes!" Twilight's mind was racing. She was trying to think of any loopholes that would stop a vortex that she could remember from her books. Of course, Twilight had never actually been in one before this, so nothing was really coming to her. She looked to Starlight Glimmer. Her student was just as much of a wreck as she. "How did this happen?"

"I was trying to solve Mooncurve's spell for you!" Starlight hollered, a pained look of embarrassment on her face. "I must have messed something up!"

"You were *what*?"

Starlight shook her head. "I knew you were worried about the hyper boosts in Ponyville! And about Game Night! And about…Comet Tail's Curse! I just…wanted you to be able to relax."

"That's very sweet of you, Starlight!" Even after all of the madness, Twilight was touched that Starlight would go to such lengths to impress her.

"Sometimes, everypony needs their own space to work and be creative. When I found this secret suite, it had everything I needed and I loved being alone in here. It even felt like it had this special energy…"

"But I don't get why you had to hide it from me…."

"For the same reason you sent me away to spend time with Sunburst!" Starlight Glimmer shot back, almost laughing. At this, Twilight began to blush. Starlight was right—she'd done the exact same thing to her student. They'd been staying away from each other. If they hadn't, they could have avoided this debacle.

"Because having time alone makes time with friends even better," Starlight said, putting her hoof down. "And that's the real way to enjoy friendship—not with a spell. Didn't you teach me that, Twilight?"

"Yes!" Twilight beamed with pride. "I did!"

Chapter

12

Dragon Knows Best

★ ★ ★

A massive gust of wind blew in, delivering Spike to the ponies' hooves. He rubbed his head and stared at the two of them upside down. "Well? Any ideas on how to stop this vortex?"

"How? We're cursed!" Twilight Sparkle

reiterated. She'd gotten so caught up in her pride for Starlight Glimmer learning friendship lessons on her own that Twilight had forgotten! "We can't use our magic."

"We've got nothing!" Starlight added. She closed her eyes and gave it an honest try. A single tiny spark sputtered from her horn. It wasn't enough magic to scratch an itch, let alone get rid of an accidental vortex. "See?"

Spike groaned and shook his head. "I can't believe you two believe in Comet Tail's Curse! That was made up by Unicorn teachers in order to get magic students to do their homework. I should know, I was there with you at school, Twilight!"

Starlight and Twilight exchanged a glance. "I thought that, too," Starlight said. "But our magic's *gone!*"

Spike sprang to his feet. "It's just magic fatigue from all the spell casting you've been doing!" He squinted his eyes and shielded them from the wind. "If you try the spell together, it will work."

It was incredibly simple, but it made sense.

"You know…I think he's right!" Twilight exclaimed with a grin. "Are you in?"

"I'm in!" Starlight nodded, eyes alight with newfound optimism.

Twilight braced herself and hoped for the best. "Ready?"

The two ponies turned to each other, closed their eyes, and recited the original spell. Immediately, everything in the room fell back to the ground, the winds stopped, and the vortex was history. Outside the front doors of the castle, the townsponies tumbled down into a large pile.

Nothing about the spell had changed, except one special ingredient. Twilight and Starlight had been working against each other the entire time, and now that they'd done it together…this time they had the power of friendship. The two ponies were finally on the same page.

"Woo-hoo! It worked!" they cheered. "We did it!"

Once the initial shock wore off, Starlight Glimmer turned to the little dragon. She raised an eyebrow at him. "When did you get to know so much about magic, Spike?"

"Since I've been hanging around a couple of supersmart wizards all the time! Wizards who were working totally differently and in a way that was not at all helpful to each other," Spike explained with a smile.

"True," Starlight said.

"But there's still one thing you two seriously need to work on as roommates..." Spike pointed to the dilapidated suite around them and laughed. "Who's gonna clean up this messy place? I really hope I don't start seeing any passive-aggressive notes around here..."

Starlight Glimmer and Twilight Sparkle burst into a fit of giggles.

"I don't think you have to worry about that," Twilight replied. "I think, from now on, our lines of communication about everypony's personal needs will be wide open." She met Starlight's eyes. "Deal?"

Starlight nodded. "Deal."

Chapter

13

The Ponyville game Night Parade

★ ★ ★

"If you wanted to host us at the castle so bad, Starlight, you should have just *told* us!" Pinkie Pie stood up and brushed herself off. Her fuchsia mane had a toy boat stuck in it. She gestured to the wreckage and crowd of very confused ponies with a giggle. "You didn't have to do all this super-speedy-super-slow-down magic to get the whole town to come over and hang out with you ponies on Game Night!"

Several ponies looked crushed. They'd been looking forward to the evening so much, and now all the work they'd put into it was ruined. Starlight felt terrible. "I'm so sorry, everypony. What a mess I've made. And for what?"

"I don't know…" Pinkie's eyes narrowed as she rubbed her chin in thought. "Unless… this was all just an elaborate surprise to start off the very first group challenge of Ponyville Game Night?!"

"Not unless the challenge is 'which pony can pick up the most litter the fastest,'"

Starlight Glimmer said and hung her head. "Not likely…"

"Hey, now! I don't see why this can't be our first challenge," Applejack replied with a shrug. "What d'ya say, ponies? This town will be back to spiffy faster than a tomcat can lick a bowl o' cream!"

A murmur of excited conversation broke out through the crowd. Soon, the towns-ponies began to nod in agreement. Some stomped their hooves on the ground.

"And we can make the grass even cleaner than before!" Fluttershy added with a sweet smile. "I know the animals would appreciate it, too."

"I'll…um…*supervise*." Rarity forced a laugh.

Applejack shot her a look.

"What? There needs to be a neutral pony to judge the competition, no?" Rarity gave an embarrassed chuckle as Applejack rolled her eyes.

"All right, Ponyville!" Applejack called out. "Let's do it!" She raised her hooves high above her cowpony hat. "On yer marks…get set… *go!*" Her hooves fell and the ponies sprang into action. It was like an odd parade mixed with a swap meet as the ponies combed the terrain, picking up items as they made their way back to the Ponyville Town Square. But everypony was having fun!

A little later, with some hoof grease and teamwork, the townsponies had soon cleaned up the Color Challenge arena. Crates were firmly back in place and water balloons were refilled. Spike and Big Mac busied themselves fixing up their gaming tables. And Fluttershy and Rainbow Dash even found the Ponyville Game Night flag and flew up to the flagpole to reattach it.

"Look, Starlight," Twilight said, picking up a sparkly yellow water balloon. "Everypony's having fun together, and it has nothing to do with spells!" She laughed as she playfully tossed the balloon at Applejack. "What was I thinking trying to use that *Mooncurve's Minutiae* in the first place?"

"And what was *I* thinking trying to practice magic in a random room that appeared out of nowhere?" Starlight replied. She cocked her head to the side. "Now that I think of it, I'm pretty sure it was one of those Andalusian Amplifiers...."

"Starlight!" Twilight gasped in astonishment. "Of *course* it was!" Her eyes were as wide as carrot cakes. "A room that amplifies everything that happens inside it... Starlight—that's why your magic was strong enough to create a vortex!" Twilight shook her head in disbelief. "It all makes sense now. An Andalusian Amplifier—in my own castle! And I didn't even know it. Wow, I really need to pay more attention to my surroundings...."

"Yeah...you do!" Starlight shrieked as she hurled a blue water balloon in Twilight's direction. The princess ducked behind a crate with a squeal of laughter as the other ponies joined in, tossing balloons at one another. Starlight Glimmer galloped to another crate, laughing as she hid from the colorful balloons.

Even with everything that had happened in the past few days, Starlight Glimmer couldn't remember another time when she'd had this much fun. It was true that a part of her wished the moment could last forever, but deep down she knew it wasn't meant to. And that was what made it pretty magical.

Dear Reader,

I put together these bonus pages just for you with my favorite new spell! Have fun filling them out and sharing them with your friends!

Magically yours,
Starlight Glimmer

THE CASTLE OF FRIENDSHIP

*Starlight Glimmer is still pretty new to
the Castle of Friendship, and she's still trying
to explore all of its twisty hallways.
Help her get down to the library in time to meet
Twilight Sparkle for a study session!*

START

FINISH

Magical Jumble

What happens when Starlight Glimmer's magic gets a little out of hand? A magical vortex, that's what! It has swirled up all of Starlight's books. Can you help rearrange the titles?

1. REATHEW MRFOSNOITA

   _ _ _ _ _ _ _ _ _ _ _ _ _ _ _ _

2. VOOMNREUC

   _ _ _ _ _ _ _ _ _

3. HAMSS TRNUEOF

   _ _ _ _ _ _ _ _ _ _ _ _

4. RTAS LWRIS

   _ _ _ _ _ _ _ _ _

YOUR OWN SECRET SUITE!

Starlight Glimmer has found a magical room that seems absolutely perfect for her to hide out and study magic! It is fully stocked with everything she needs, and decorated just the way she likes. What would you put in your special room? Write down some ideas here!

_____

_____

_____

_____

_____

_____

_____

_____

Now draw your secret suite!

SAY THE MAGIC WORDS

Can you find the words in the puzzle below and help Starlight finish her spell? The words may be horizontal, vertical, diagonal, or even backward!

H	L	U	T	D	S	M	N	V	L
P	Y	H	C	C	P	V	R	O	C
C	A	P	O	G	E	Q	O	R	M
L	R	M	E	T	L	P	C	T	C
E	E	A	U	R	L	Q	I	E	S
T	M	N	D	F	B	M	N	X	D
Z	I	I	P	X	O	O	U	J	H
M	X	K	T	X	O	N	O	T	N
C	I	G	A	M	K	Q	F	S	E
S	D	N	E	I	R	F	X	Z	T

**COMET   FRIENDS   HYPER BOOST
MAGIC   MINUTE   SPELL BOOK
TIME   UNICORN   VORTEX**

SPELL WRITING 101

Twilight Sparkle and Starlight Glimmer are trying their hardest to rewrite a spell so each minute they spend with their friends seems like it lasts longer. Can you write your own rhyming spell? What does it do?

_____

_____

_____

_____

_____

_____

_____

_____

_____

HYPER BOOST HYSTERIA!

*Oh no! There's been another hyper boost,
and everypony is rushing through their day
at super-fast speeds! Use the space below to list
the things you would like to speed up.*

_____

_____

_____

_____

_____

_____

_____

_____

_____

Draw what your friends would look like if they were caught in a hyper boost right now!

RHYME TIME!

Starlight Glimmer is having a tough time finding the right rhyming words to finish a spell. Can you help her match the words that rhyme with one another?

EXTEND	HOURGLASS
SCHEME	SEEM
PRESERVE	FRIEND
SECOND	RECKONED
OVERPASS	MOONCURVE

MAGICAL MIX-UP!

The time stream is completely messed up!
Write down the order of the events below to
put Starlight Glimmer's story right!

..... Starlight finds a secret room and
locks it from the inside.

..... Starlight creates a magical vortex.

..... Everypony slows down before
Game Night.

..... Twilight Sparkle suggests Starlight
go to the Crystal Empire.

..... Twilight and Starlight study together.

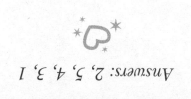

Answers: 2, 5, 4, 3, 1

FULL-ON FRIENDSHIP

Starlight Glimmer is learning how to be the best friend she can be to Twilight Sparkle, but she's not quite ready to be spending so much time together. She doesn't want to hurt Twilight's feelings, so she pretends she's too tired to hang out. Write about a time when you had to make sure you weren't hurting a good friend's feelings. How did it work?

_____

_____

_____

_____

_____

_____

GAME NIGHT!

*Everypony's favorite event,
Ponyville Game Night, is coming up!
List some of your very favorite games
to play with your own friends!*

_____

_____

_____

_____

_____

_____

_____

_____

Twice the Twilight

One of Starlight Glimmer's new spells has gone mega-haywire, and now there's another Twilight Sparkle running around the Castle! Help Starlight spot the five differences between the two and find the real Twilight to reverse the spell.

FRiENDS AND FAMiLY

NOW ON DVD!

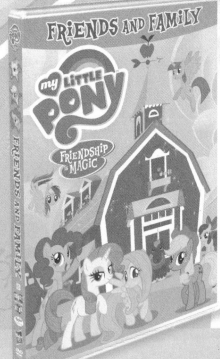